This book belongs to:

_____

MERRY CHRISTMAS, PETER!

FREDERICK WARNE
Published by the Penguin Group
Penguin Group (USA) LLC, 375 Hudson Street, New York, New York 10014, USA

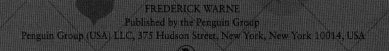

USA | Canada | UK | Ireland | Australia | New Zealand | India | South Africa | China

penguin.com
A Penguin Random House Company

ISBN 978-0-14-135173-5
10 9 8 7 6 5 4 3 2

MERRY CHRISTMAS, PETER!

F. WARNE & CO.

It was Christmas Eve, and Peter, Benjamin, and Lily were setting off on a very important mission.

"I need you to go to the store and buy Christmas presents for everyone in the woods," said Mrs. Rabbit.

"You can count on us, Mom," said Peter.

"Deliver them as quickly as you can and get home before dark," Mrs. Rabbit continued. "And watch out for that sneaky Mr. Tod."

"We will," said Peter. "Come on, let's hop to it!"

"WOOOO HOOOO!"

cried the three bunnies, as the sled
whooshed down the snowy slope.

The friends were having so much fun they forgot all about the time, and about their important mission.

Suddenly Lily looked up at the darkening sky. "It's getting late!" she said, worried. "We better get to the store before it closes."

They arrived just in time.

"Phew, I hope there's room for everything on
the sled!" Peter said, as the friends carried out the
presents they'd bought.

"Next stop—sky-high Squirrel Camp for the first delivery!" declared Lily.

The rabbits didn't notice Mr. Tod lurking outside the store.

"Hello!" called Peter, when they arrived at the squirrels' secret hideout. "Anybody up there?"

"Maybe they're not here," said Benjamin.

"They're hiding," whispered Peter. "Whatever you do, don't say . . . snowball fight."

"SNOWBALL FIGHT?" Lily repeated, loudly.

"Did somebody say
'SNOWBALL FIGHT'?"
yelled Squirrel Nutkin.

The bunnies dived for cover, as Nutkin
and his band of cheeky squirrels pelted
them with snowballs.

"We'd love to play, Nutkin," Peter laughed, handing Nutkin his gift, "but we've got to dash."

"Merry Christmas!" called Lily, as the friends set off on their sled again.

The sky was getting darker still, as snow started to fall.
"I know a great shortcut," said Peter, steering the
sled down a steep hill and weaving in and out of the trees.

As they sped faster and faster, the heavy sled creaked under
the strain.

"Watch out!" shouted Lily.

"Peeeeeter!"
cried Benjamin, closing his eyes tightly.

"WHOA!"

the friends yelled as the sled hit a bump.
The rabbits tumbled into the snow, with
the presents all around them. And the sled
rattled on . . . straight onto an icy lake.

Peter, Benjamin, and Lily watched in horror as . . .

CRAAACK!

. . . the ice broke and the sled slid into the icy water.

"This is bad. This is really bad," groaned Benjamin.

"How will we deliver the presents now?" asked Lily.

Looking around, Peter saw that they were right by Mr. McGregor's garden. "A good rabbit never gives up," he declared.

"And I've got a tip-top idea. Follow me!"

Inside the garden, the friends found garden canes, string, and Mr. McGregor's broken old wheelbarrow.

"Nice work," said Peter, standing back to admire their super new sled.

"Perfect," said Lily, piling the Christmas goodies inside.

But as they set off again, the sled was pulled out from under the startled bunnies . . .

"MR. TOD!" they gasped.

"Peter Rabbit," said Mr. Tod, flashing a toothy grin.
"You and your little friends can join me for a
Christmas feast!"

"Um, maybe another time," replied Peter, desperately looking for a way to escape.

"But it's been so long since I had rabbit . . . I mean, friends . . . for dinner!" said the fearsome fox, licking his lips.

"Try a snowball instead!"

cried Peter, scooping up a paw-full of snow and hurling
it at Mr. Tod—**SPLAT!**

"Oh dear," sighed Mr. Tod, sarcastically.
"Is that the best you can do?"

Peter, Lily, and Benjamin
threw more snowballs.

"Bah, stop that," said the fox, starting to get annoyed.
"I don't want a . . ."

"Come on, say it," Peter whispered under his breath, taking aim again.

"SNOWBALL FIGHT!"

shouted Mr. Tod, as Peter's snowball hit him right on the nose.

Mr. Tod's words echoed around the woods . . .

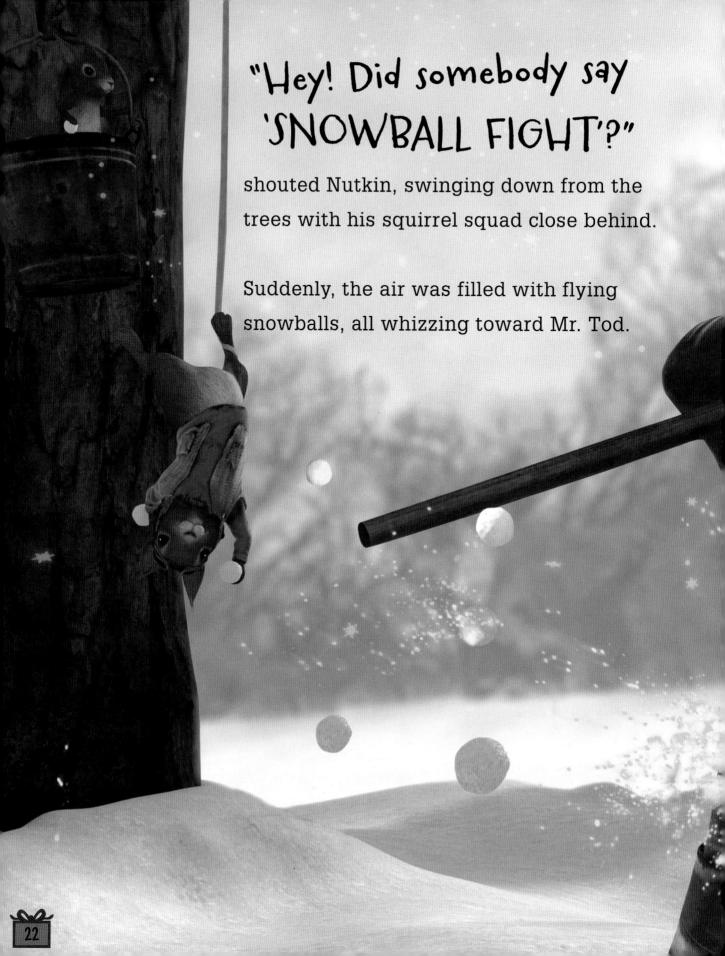

"Hey! Did somebody say 'SNOWBALL FIGHT'?"

shouted Nutkin, swinging down from the trees with his squirrel squad close behind.

Suddenly, the air was filled with flying snowballs, all whizzing toward Mr. Tod.

"Ouch! Ow! Hey!"
shouted the flustered fox.
"This isn't fair!"

Mr. Tod ran away, snowballs flying after him.

"Now that's what I call friends in high places!" said Peter.

"Thanks, Nutkin."

It was snowing heavily now, and night was starting to fall. Peter found the sled half-buried in snow. Together, they all tried to pull it out, but . . .

"It won't budge," panted Benjamin.

"We've got to get this sled moving," urged Peter. **"Everyone's depending on us!"**

"I have an idea," said Lily, looking at Nutkin and the squirrels. She reached into her Just-in-Case Pocket and pulled out some elastic bands.

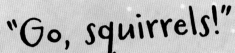

"Go, squirrels!"

cheered Lily, as the sled raced
across the snow, pulled by
Nutkin and his cheeky chums.

"Hey, this is fun!" called Nutkin, pinging on the springy elastic reins.

"We'll make those deliveries
in next to no time!"
cried Peter.

"Merry Christmas, Mr. Fisher!"

called Benjamin, as they quickly dropped off Mr. Fisher's present.

"A gift for you, Mrs. Tiggy-winkle!"

cheered Lily, as the sled sped on.

"Oh, thank you!" gasped Jemima Puddle-duck, hugging the rabbits happily. **"And Merry Christmas to you!"**

The presents all had been delivered. It was time to say good-bye to the squirrels and head home.

Late on Christmas Eve, family and friends gathered in the cozy burrow. Peter, Benjamin, and Lily told everyone about their snowy adventure.

"**Well done!**" said Mrs. Rabbit proudly. "Thanks to you, everyone will have a wonderful Christmas."

"It's going to be the best ever!" Peter smiled.

"Merry Christmas, everyone!"